THE GIFT

Cover illustrated by Rusty Fletcher

Illustrated by Debbie Dieneman

Adapted by Jennifer Boudart

Louis Weber, C.E.O.
Publications International, Ltd.
7373 North Cicero Avenue
Lincolnwood, Illinois 60712

www.pubint.com

Manufactured in China.

8 7 6 5 4 3 2 1

ISBN: 0-7853-7877-4

Percy and Amelia were twin bear cubs. That meant that the brother and sister shared the same birthday. They shared almost everything, even their playtime. They loved being outdoors. Percy loved to fly the kite his father helped him make. He had even tied the kite's tail himself.

Amelia loved looking through her binoculars. They had been a gift from her Aunt Ruth. The binoculars hung around Amelia's neck wherever she went. When she was outside, she was always searching trees and hilltops through her trusty binoculars. Percy's eyes were always on his kite as it danced in the sky.

One day, Percy stood at the edge of the forest, holding the kite's string in his hands. When he would pull back the string, the kite would jump through the air. The kite's streaming tail twisted back and forth in the breeze. Percy knew to keep his toy away from the trees. He had climbed more than a few trees to rescue the kite from branches.

The kite's tail was now torn and a bit muddy. Sometimes the knots came loose. In fact, the tail wasn't as long as it used to be. Once it had gotten stuck in a bush. When that happened, Percy had to cut off part of the tail. He did his very best to patch it up. It was the only kite tail he had. Only his care had kept the old kite flying.

Amelia sometimes pretended that she was a nature explorer. She used her binoculars to spot the birds hiding among the leaves. One day she saw three beautiful birds. Amelia pretended that they were rare African eagles.

Because she looked through her binoculars so much, Amelia saw a lot of things that others probably missed. That was one reason they were so special to her. Every night Amelia cleaned off her binoculars and polished the glass lenses with great care. Then she slipped the special binoculars  underneath her pillow. It was the only safe place she could think of to keep them.

The day before their birthday, Amelia sat alone in the room she shared with Percy. Their birthday was the next day. She had found the perfect gift: a brand new tail for his kite. It was longer than the homemade tail had ever been. This new tail would keep Percy's kite flying high for many years.

Amelia started saving her money the first day she saw the kite tail in the shop. She hoped she had enough saved now to buy it. Amelia emptied her bank and counted the coins. She did not have enough money to buy the gift! Amelia stretched out on her bed and thought. Suddenly she had an idea!

Amelia raced to the shop. She went to the checkout counter. "Can I help you, young lady?" asked the shopkeeper.

"I sure hope so," answered Amelia, setting down the binoculars. "Would you buy these?"

The shopkeeper looked them over. He rubbed his beard and said, "I think we can make a deal." He handed Amelia a big pile of crisp dollar bills. Right away she used the money to buy Percy's gift. She even had enough left over to buy special wrapping paper. On her way home, Amelia held the gift close to her. She thought about how the binoculars used to feel when she walked. She would miss them, but her brother was worth it.

Percy walked to the shop after he had spent the day flying his kite. He found the perfect gift for his sister: a carrying case for her binoculars. The case was lined with velvet and had a lock and key. "Now," he thought, "Amelia will have a safe place to store her binoculars." Percy didn't have money for the gift, but he had a plan. He walked up to the shopkeeper at the front counter. "I want to sell my kite," announced Percy.

The shopkeeper looked it over. "Well, it needs a new tail, but I can fix that," he said. They made a deal, and Percy left with the gift tucked under his arm. He used to carry his kite that way. Percy would miss the kite, but his sister was worth it.

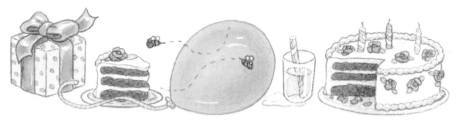

Finally it was the day of the party. Amelia was excited but nervous, too. She could not wait for Percy to open the gift she had found for him. But what if he found out she had sold her binoculars? Would he get upset? She would just have to tell him he was the best kite flyer in the world, and he should have the best kite tail ever. It made her happy do something nice for him.

When Amelia walked in the front door, Percy was waiting for her. Amelia smiled at her brother and shouted out, "Happy birthday, Percy!"

"Happy birthday, Amelia!" Percy shouted back.

Amelia and Percy blew out the
candles and ate some cake. Finally
it was time to open up the presents.
Ripping open the wrapping paper,
they were very surprised at what was inside. Percy
didn't want Amelia to know about the kite, so he
said, "Get your binoculars and try out the case!"

Amelia didn't want Percy to know about her
binoculars. "Don't you just love your new kite tail?
I just had to buy it for you. Go get your kite!"

Percy sighed out loud. Then he said, "Amelia,
I'm so sorry. I sold the kite to buy your gift."

Now Amelia's mouth dropped open. "I'm
sorry, too. I sold my binoculars to buy your gift!"

The twins laughed and laughed at what had happened. When they could finally stop laughing, they said to each other, "I just wanted you to be happy!" Then they hugged each other.

"I think trying to make someone happy is the best gift of all," said their mom. "Don't forget, you still have other gifts to open."

"I know," said Amelia, "let's finish our party outside. We'll take our presents and cake to the forest for a picnic!"

The twins packed the picnic basket and went to find the perfect spot for their birthday picnic. They had a great time. Amelia and Percy agreed it was the best birthday they ever had.

One to Grow On

Generosity

Generosity is about giving to others without thinking of yourself. Amelia and Percy were very generous. Their love for each other made it easy to part with something that meant a lot to them.

In this story Percy and Amelia remind us that being generous is rewarding. Can you think of a time when someone was generous to you? Can you think of ways to show generosity?